INTERTWISTED

Talia Louise Mclavy

This book is a work of fiction. Names, characters, business, organizations, medical advice, places and events other than those clearly in the public domain, are either the product of the author's imagination or are used fictitiously.

Copyright © 2024 Talia Louise Mclavy

ISBN: 9798342408264

All rights reserved. No part of this book may be reproduced or used in any manner without the prior written permission of the copyright owner, except for the use of brief quotations in a book review.

To request permission, contact the owner at
taliapowell1234@hotmail.com

INTERTWISTED

Talia Louise Mclavy

Dedication

To everyone who has heard me say "one day I will write a book".

I did it.

Chapter One

In 2022, a 35 year old woman was found dead outside her home. A key piece of evidence was a diary submitted by St Elim Hospital, detailing the events involved.

A 35 year old man, named Oliver Tamsin, provided a statement.

This is their story.

Chapter Two

Him

Do you know how it feels to lose someone you have an inexplicable bond with?

Someone, whose entire soul and sole existence weaves around your own – unable to exist without you, and you them. Someone who shares the pulse running through your veins, whose heart beats in pace with your own, and whose dreams are so tightly intertwined with yours, that you can barely tell them apart?

I do.

I lost her.

Chapter Three

Him

When I first heard news of the accident, it was a normal day. 'Normal' is never what I had dreamed of doing, but somehow I had slipped into the mundanity of it all, like everybody else. Coffee at 7am. Train by 8. The monotonously steady beat of my polished shoes on the concrete walk to work provides the gloomy soundtrack to my morning life. Me, in the starring role, playing the dutiful part of a career man amongst a crowd of like minded suits. Newspaper by 8.20am from the local paper shop, less to read and more to act as a conversation barrier between me and anyone daring enough to say hello. Mindless chit chat to the cashier until 8.30am. Then the final push of pace to the office for 8.45am. It was all a prerequisite to nothingness. As if I was in any sort of rush to reach the soulless, mind numbing constraint of my desk job. Some days I would pray to get hit by a bus on the way in, just so something different would happen and I would actually FEEL something.

It kept me sane: my routine. That solitary hour before work was like Schrodinger's cat; in that hour lay the possibility that the day could be full of excitement, of challenge, of wonder. Or it could, again, be full of the predictable ooze that penetrated every orifice as the clock ticked by, getting more and more suffocating every day. Why I thought starting the day in the same way would bring about any different results is beyond me. But now I realise now there was comfort in the predictable.

It wasn't supposed to be like this: my life. When Her and I used to talk about our future, I never imagined a monotonous drudge. It had all seemed so bright - I would be wearing trendy glasses with fashionable shirts and hold a penchant for being quirky, using air quotes and slang as a part of my daily repertoire. I'd be "the boss" but with a relaxed, calming approach, dripping with natural authority that never had to be forced. My colleagues would listen to me out of respect for being too young and too cool for my bloated career achievements and we would brainstorm around a table designed by the Swedish, shooting out ideas, relaxed, trendy, ingenious. I would stand out. I would thrive.

When She envisioned her future, her goals changed by the day and nothing seemed to stick but the excitement was always palpable - the only consistency in her inconsistent dreams. Her desires and ambitions were as beautifully erratic and ever changing as she was. First it was the year travelling around Europe that she could never quite afford. Then it was the yoga teaching qualification that never got finished. Then the painting that lost momentum after a hefty purchase of all of the expensive art gear, just to collect dust in the spare room. The only constant became the years of waitressing, flirting, watching and taking orders and the nights she came home, feet aching, clothes smelling of smoke and grease. My only role was to hug her and tell her it would be worth it someday. We were all about ambition. Until life got in the way.

I remember that morning, as if the memory is stamped underneath my eyelids. It was my 5 year anniversary with The Company. The company I had initially joined optimistically as a stop gap, to kick start my funds for the start-up dream. The company she and I had mocked for being "grey" in every sense of the word. Grey walls, grey desk, grey suits. Even the faces of the staff were grey washed with boredom. We had laughed on my first day at how I was so *different* from the usual employees that scattered around the office like identical seeds of corn, pale and lifeless, small and unimpressive, yet to grow into anything worth consuming. Back then, I felt like a shiny fire streaked fox amongst the pigeons that pecked mindlessly at their desks, living and dying by the pecking order. Peck peck peck. Five years of greyness, repairing broken keyboards and rebooting frozen systems and now I was the one frozen.

That morning was normal. I had waved to Helen at reception on my way in. I had laughed, as was dutiful to do, at the sickening baby blue balloons that littered my desk as cheap appreciation of my 5 year sentence. I had shaken hands with Carl, my boss, as he thanked me for my service, one eye on his iphone barely finishing his sentence before the disinterest kicked in.. Peck peck peck. It was all set to be another, boring day. 5 years, less of a celebration and more of an embarrassment.

Then 9.35am arrived and my world turned upside down.

An accident. And Her.

And then all of the grey turned black.

Chapter Four

Her Diary: Entry 1

Chapter Five

Him

The news had arrived in the form of a phone call to the office. I rarely recieved phone calls at work. I would hardly say I was a social butterfly - Yes I had a mobile phone and social media, but it always seemed so embarrassing to use and post anything that wasn't overwhelmingly underwhelming - I could just about face the boredom of my life myself, let alone subject it to the masses adorned with a sickening filter, only to revel in the lack of engagement. My mobile phone spent most of my day in my pocket, save for the occasional text and the check of my share prices and the company didn't provide landlines on our desk, unless you had "an office" - a detail I found comforting when wanting to escape from constant ringing of human interaction that usually came with a work phone. Not so great if anybody on the outside of The Company wanted to contact you during working hours and you weren't glued to your mobile phone.

I had sat there for only 30 minutes that morning, pecking away at the keyboard, answering some monotonous email question that could have been googled by them and saved my fingertips from the excruciating effort, when Helen from reception had ambled over to my desk. A large lady. Blonde, but not natural. Fingernails always slightly too long and painted bright red. She was an attractive woman, even if she was on the wrong side of overweight and the only thing she put more effort in than her appearance, was her work. She was known for her crocodile wide smile and a penchant for "not leaving the desk unless absolutely necessary" (more from laziness than efficiency) and taking her job as seriously as the colour of her lips that morning: deep maroon.

"Oliver" She had drawled, looking impatient at having to slump across the floor for the 2 minute walk from reception to my desk. 2 minutes there and 2 minutes back. That was 4 minutes 'her' reception would be left unattended. I could see the annoyance written across that maroon mask, although her elastic smile was stretched to the point of snapping. "There's a phone call for you on line 3. Some posh sounding woman. Says it's urgent. You best come."

Some posh woman. That had amused me at the time. If it was Her, she would relish the thought of being called posh, perfecting her phone voice over our years together. She had put it into play numerous times, calling into college to cover for me when we had decided that going to see a black and white French film that day was "much better for our education" than four hours of classes or telling work I was run down with a bout of "dysentery" after copious gin drinking the night before. We were far from posh, but the faceless pretence of an eloquent phone call was easy to convince the listener otherwise. She would be proud of such an assumption. She loved a facade.

I spent the first minute of the walk smiling to myself over this titbit and allowing myself to reminisce. It wasn't until the last ten seconds, reception in my direct line of sight, that my humour changed to confusion as to why she would even be calling me at reception. She knew better. My pace visibly quickened and so did my heart rate.

"Hello?" I had questioned, my body draped over Helens desk in order to reach the receiver from the other side of the counter. Under no circumstances could you go behind Helens desk, we had all been told various times. That was for Helen and Helen alone.

"Mr Tamsin?" The voice had replied. Posh? Yes. Her? No. I didn't recognise the voice. "Yes" was all I could reply, the word quick and staccato like a gunshot fired from my throat, unwilling to put any more time between myself and the answer.

"Mr Tamsin this is PC Susan Harp at Letherington Station. I'm afraid to tell you that Cecelia was involved in an accident this morning. She is currently in intensive care. Unresponsive but alive. We need you to make arrangements immediately to attend. Is this possible?" Her formal tone was clipped. Machine like. Professional.

I stood there, the cold groove of the counter digging into the pit of my stomach; the only thing stopping me from hitting the ground. I remember the incessant tapping of Helen's nails on the counter as she impatiently waited for me to wrap up the call, oblivious to the darkness unfolding on the other end of the line. I remember the thudding of my heart as I digested what I'd been told.

I hung up and within 4 minutes I was out of that door.

Chapter Six

Her Diary - Entry 2

Hello. My name is Cecelia Tamsin.

I don't know who I am or what has happened.

Chapter Seven

Him

An accident. Hot oil. Physical disfigurement. Facial injuries. Severe.

I had called the hospital from the car and the words had swum around my head looking for meaning, ricocheting off each temple. The taxi ride to the hospital was excruciating, with a Taxi driver persisting to vomit conversational niceties through the cold glass that tangibly separated us, his humdrum singalong voice, an advertisement that he had no care in the world, separated us in a completely different way. "Good day lad'?" He had whistled through the pane, focused solely on his ambition for a 5 star uber rating that he failed to read the nausea on my face. I mumbled some incoherent response that could pass as a full stop at the end of this sentencing conversation, my palms sweating and stomach turning quicker than the numbers on his metre. I had to wait until I got to the hospital for more information and did not intend to spend that limbo time limboing around pleasantries with a complete stranger.

I remember the battery on my mobile phone flashing below 20% while we meandered through traffic, and thinking how pointless that lump of metal would be should it drain to zero. She had thought it a good idea to get one, in order for us to communicate more, but I found the whole notion of being instantly detectable suffocating, particularly by her. She used to mock me, for being a "technology guy" but hating most technology. 'It's not technology I hate darling – it's communication" I would say. It was only at times like these that I wished I was more forthcoming with others on the connection front. I had never felt more alone than when the taxi swam into the visitors bay.

That day, the hospital felt familiar, although I had never been to this one before, I had been to plenty over the years. I always empathised with the entrance to a hospital; the silver sliding doors pulling reluctantly open to reveal dread and emptiness inside. As if they wanted to stay closed and hold all the sadness in but were forced to open up over and over and receive the babbling, chaotic visitors that wanted to charge down the aisles. I could relate. I immediately questioned my ability to go inside, feeling so fragile that a gust of wind could blow my conviction away and set me back at work, a mere 30 minutes before when none of this had happened.

But I didn't. This time I entered. I questioned. I waited. But then I left.

Chapter Eight

Her Diary Entry 3

Who Am I?

Chapter Nine

Him

Facing fear is something I have struggled with my entire life, being much more accustomed to burying my head in the sand, or choosing the road which is not less travelled, but less difficult to travel. I always took the easy way out.

In college once, one of my friends, Nicky, called me a "people pleaser". At the time I had taken it as a compliment - that my gang considered me someone that made them pleased; always considering other people, happy go lucky, agreeable. Reveling in the fact that people thought I would bend over backwards for others - it made me feel angelic, selfless, a real saint. Good old Oliver. Always going with the flow and happy to help. In actual fact, the people pleasing came less from a need to make others happy, and more of an innate driven passion to prevent me from feeling uncomfortable. Selflessness was my ultimately selfish act. Conflict made me nauseous and I would do *everything* to avoid it, including agreeing to things I didn't want to do, just so I wouldn't "rock the boat". I couldn't care less about anyone else's happiness, as long as they weren't affecting mine, and mine was driven from the ability to maintain a quiet life.

She was much less agreeable than I was and completely comfortable with losing her temper and cherishing anybody that would enter a heated debate and challenge her intellect - the more challenging the better. She always got satisfaction from winning, and the tougher the debate, the sweeter the satisfaction became. She always saw conflict as growth, an opportunity to learn and better yourself from the challenge. I always saw conflict as a nightmare. One I would avoid at all costs. Even the cost of myself.

After seeing her in intensive care that day, I felt like a part of me had been stripped away. Blood has dried across her frail body, plastering her hair to her skin like suffocating candle wax, her clothes wound tightly around her like she was swaddled in despair, her eyes closed as if she too could barely even look at herself. Permanent disfigurement. Severe facial burns. The words swam around me, the pressure slamming against my ears and sitting on my chest. I had a sickening urge to leave, to get out, to push it to the back of my mind and pretend it wasn't happening and for the first time in my life had longed for the comfort of my grey desk - but my legs were weighted down with the severity of it all and were unable to move. There she was, like the physical manifestation of the pain I felt within my heart; ragged, torn and irreparable.

I remember when we were younger, at the age of 22 she sat me down and told me for the first time that she was thinking of leaving to go travelling. She wanted to "find herself", she said. She had spent too long being a part of "us" and wanted to be "her" for a while. She knew it was never something I could or would do, it was beyond the realms of my personality and it had broken my heart, that my other half wanted to leave, and leave me behind. I had painted on a smile, played the supportive role and buried my head, praying her flakiness would kick in quicker than normal and the whole idea would dissipate into another pipe dream. She was always the more flamboyant of the two of us. I was always the steady one, both ambitious, but in different ways. She was always driven, spontaneous, life grabbing. I was quiet, sensitive, and broody. In the end she decided not to go. She had decided not to leave me. I knew she wouldn't. We could never bare to be apart for long.

But it took a single conversation with a nurse that day to change everything - Cecelia would need urgent care and would be immediately taken into surgery. I was ushered abruptly into a waiting room while she was wheeled at pace into the bright lights of the theatre and suddenly, hope suspended, being alone felt like the only option.

So I left.

Being a coward is not something you can turn off for long.

Chapter Ten

Her Diary Entry 4

Hello diary. Hello hello hello,

What the hell am I supposed to write here? It seems a bit silly to start DEAR DIARY, as if it's a person, I don't even know myself let alone who this diary is! But I have to write something all the same. So what can I say?

I am probably the ugliest person alive.

That's dramatic. But it's how I feel. I looked in the mirror this morning, and the red oozing wound from just under my eye to the top of my shoulder blade is disgusting - the only evidence for me to believe an accident even happened. I feel like whoever I am has been blocked out in my mind by a big white space of emptiness. I have no idea who I am, what I do, where I live, or what happened to get me here. "It will come back to you Cecelia" the medical professionals told me. "Give yourself time to recover".

I hope it heals. I can see a life of balaclavas, turtlenecks and scarves staring back at me from my future. Maybe I could just constantly wear a mask on the one side of my face, that goes from crown to collarbone. If that fails I can just stay hidden behind closed doors watching nauseating day time tv all day. The phantom of the soap opera. Ha ha.

So the nurses have told me to start this diary, somewhat against my will. My first entry was artistic I think, but they tell me that's not good enough. I need to "open up" and invest time into this, in order to make sense of what's happened. To say that my memory has turned into mincemeat is an understatement. Oh, ask me about what happened yesterday, and what happened the day before, and the day before, and I'm good to go. (They all involve me laying in this hospital bed, sleeping, hardly anything to write home about!). But ask me about anything that happened before that, and it's like a big black doorstop is wedged in the way of the door to my past. Nothing. "Write a diary" they said. "It will help you remember" they said. Hmm.

NOTHING YET.

Apparently, the nurses can't just "tell" me about the accident, in detail, as per my request, as it may induce some sort of prolonged shock that it seems could result in me jabbing this drip needle into both my eyes. Apparently. That's me paraphrasing. So here I am, writing this diary, in a hospital room with a man old enough to be my grandfather sitting opposite me in his own bed, who IS actually annoying enough to possibly justify the drip needle to his eye. That's harsh. I hope the nurses don't ask to read this. He's old and recovering from some sort of injury He spoke to me twice; another reason that forced me write this diary and "look busy" before he trolls me with more tales of the war and "in my day".

So let's start with what I DO know. I know my name (they told me!) Cecelia Tamsin. I know I work (worked?) in a restaurant in the middle of town. I know the year. I know the date. I know I was in an accident two days ago and now I am on day three of what they are sickeningly calling my "recovery".

I also know, I haven't had a visitor since I woke up. 3 days. What sort of person doesn't have visitors?

Chapter Eleven

Him

My mother always told me I had issues with adapting to change and looking back, it seems she was more right than I ever gave her credit for. "Walk the path less travelled" Cecelia had once said to me. I was happy not walking anywhere at all. I was always happy to stay put, stay in my lane, stay in my comfort zone - any changes making me freeze inside. When problems arose, I *definitely* didn't have any Fight or Flight within me - I would stay frozen, rooted to the spot, unable to move. Its the one consistent trait in my life that's kept me stuck all of these years -both bored and comforted by the mundane. And when trouble arose, the safest place for me was my own shell, retreating into silence, comforted by my 'normal'. I couldn't handle pressure. I couldn't handle change. I definitely couldn't handle Cecelia.

I read somewhere once about how having an unstable upbringing, in a volatile home, shapes your behaviour for the rest of your life and as self-awareness slaps you in the face when you hit 30 I now tended to agree. When things become too real for me, or too big to handle, I know I shut down to protect myself. To keep myself safe. I could cut off all of my emotions, compartmentalise them, rearrange them like playdough until they lost all feeling and became what I needed them to be. Its the only way I learned how to cope. I never gave my mother enough credit for that either.

But its so surprising what a good looking suit, a clean shave, and a polished pair of shoes can do to cover what is actually inside. "Oliver is such a nice guy" everybody would always say. "So grounded". "So laid back". I would always simultaneously wince and celebrate this assumption - happy that I wasn't rocking the boat, embarrassed that that's all I had become. Pleased that I was successfully portraying how I wanted the world to see me. But behind closed doors was another story.

Because the first three days after the accident, I spent them in bed with Amala.

Her legs wrapped around me protectively, my face smothered in her thick black hair to block out the noise. I had practically ran to her as soon as I left the hospital.

Do you know how hard it is to see your other half, someone you have shared all of your life with, reduced to a battered, burnt mess? It may have been selfish, given the circumstances, but I had a gaping hole within me that opened on the day of the accident and it needed to be filled.

Amala had always been good at that. She knew the relationship with myself and Cecelia was erratic and she was usually happy to look the other way, keeping well out of any conversations that involved Cecelia. Amala was always good for comfort and prided herself on my relaxation and always seemed ambivalent to the existence of Cecelia, as long as it didn't impact when we were together - a deal I was always happy to indulge. Amala was a goddess to me. I was lucky to have her in whatever capacity I could.

It was on day four that I finally bit the bullet and went back to the hospital.

These things have a way of catching up with you

Chapter Twelve

Her Diary - Entry 5

Hello Diary, it's me. (who else would it be.)

Officially four days since the accident. Two days asleep, now two days awake. Tomorrow will officially tip the scale forward where consciousness in this hospital bed outweighs my vegetative state. Although I still feel like a potato, lying in this bed. A couch potato. I don't understand why the nurses won't let me get up and go outside. I could still be a potato there, just one covered in sunlight, given a chance to grow. I need stimulation. I'll turn into a pile of soggy mash at this rate. Much like my memory. It still isn't improving.

Day four (As today is officially known) IS however, the day where I finally get a visitor through those doors. The nurses gave me the news very delicately, as if it would break me - it was the best news I have had since arriving! (Ha - arriving, as if it was an event I had RSVP'd to.)

Oliver, they tell me. I could see them scanning my face for any sort of recognition when they announced his name, the nurses left eye twitching every so slightly to concentrate hard on my reaction, but I have absolutely no idea and that scares me to death. I don't want to show them the fear though, I can't deal with any emotional pity as well as the physical pity at my deformed face.

But It IS scary that I have absolutely no idea of who is to arrive. "Oliver Tamsin, meet Cecelia Tamsin. She doesn't have a clue who you are." A charming sentiment. However, currently, fear is being masked with annoyance at why it's taken four excruciating days to get someone through that door. 'Tamsin'. Same surname as me. I refuse to ask the nurses, I can't deal with them talking to me like I'm a baby.

For the record - Hospitals are horrible places. It's like the doctors went to an interior designer and asked for "Bleak". "Oh I can do bleak!" they announce, flitting around, all coat tails and frilly shirts. "I'm thinking floors as cold as bodies and walls as dim as their future! I think Dulux does a colour called "ultimate depression": perfect!"

On a different note, the nurses DID try and read this bloody diary. I told them initially that I would only do it if it was private and the young one with the mousy hair had smiled and agreed with me, but I saw her trying to leaf through as I stirred from yesterday's nap. The stack of old TV Guides on the communal table are clearly not satisfying enough for her perusal. She's quite welcome to read this if she so wishes, but I would like permission to be asked first - there's nothing in here of any substance. She probably knows more about me than I do.

Anyway, 2pm is visitor time they tell me. I need to somewhat make myself presentable.

Chapter Thirteen

Him

Have you ever dealt with the feeling that you HAVE to do something, but the urgency and motivation is totally eclipsed by a complete and utter reluctance to get it done. An essay for example, with a looming deadline. I would always wait right up until a day before it was due to be handed in, and then, when there was no longer any wiggle room left for me to procrastinate into, I would dutifully get it done, anxiety levels through the rough, disheartened by the substandard quality. If there was time, I had time, I would tell myself, allowing the problem that could have been easily solved with minimal stress within a lengthy time frame, suddenly maximised to the hilt with no time left to spare.

This is how visiting Cecelia felt. As long as I was with Amala, that alternate hideous reality didn't exist. It was just me and her and nothing else existed outside of the four walls. I could convince myself that it wasn't happening and that nothing else mattered. I could lock myself away behind a door of safety. But before long, reality always comes knocking and it's even harder to ignore the banging on the door.

Four days it took for me to drag myself back through those double doors at the hospital, 8 missed calls from the nurses and I had picked up on the ninth, brushing off their judgemental tones of "we have been trying to contact you", hoping they wouldn't mention it again after I mumbled something akin to a broken phone. Thankfully, It seemed they were as disgusted by my absence as I expected and were reluctant to enhance the disgust with further probing, seemingly just glad I had finally answered, the agitation shrouded underneath forceful cloak of professionalism. An urgent visit was required, they had said. No other visitors had visited, they said - had I contacted her friends and family? Obviously not. Her friends were as scattered as she was, collected like mismatched memorabilia from various retreats, concerts and communities that I would dare not ever entertain let alone contact any family? That dissipated a long time ago. It was just me.

I hadn't returned to work since the accident, of which the company "completely understood" as "I needed to spend time with Cecelia". None of them were aware that I hadn't spent a single moment with her in my three days of leave so far. "Oliver is such a nice guy" they had said. "Couldn't have happened to a nicer bloke".

Gripping onto this outside perception of me was even harder when I arrived at the hospital. It was clear that within those three days, things had gotten somewhat better, but also tremendously worse. A quick medical brief from the nurses told me that She was struggling to remember anything before the accident; who she was, who I was, what had happened. They asked me to be mindful of this and to not bombard her with details to overwhelm and scare her. Her treatment is delicate, they said. They didn't yet know that I wasn't the bombarding type. They asked me to hand over my phone and remove my personal belongings, including my wedding ring, on entry - "lets not give her reason to ask any questions yet" they had said. "We want to ease her into remembrance Mr Tamsin. Allow her to unveil your identity on her own. She is struggling with the fact that for 3 days nobody has been here". The guilt of that statement alone had made me comply.

The plan, or so they told me, was to "just spend some time with her", alone in her hospital room, to gently see if I could make any progress with her memory and recovery. I was to ask no questions, give answers gently only when asked and offer comfort where possible - I suppose the nurses were hoping that one look at me would snap something inside Cecelia and bring it all back. I was praying not a single god damn thing within Cecelia would snap. Because nobody would be prepared for what could happen if it did.

Chapter Fourteen

Her Diary, Entry 6

I can not write properly. My hands wont keep up with how fast my brain is going. An hour ago he was here and for the first time in days, I FEEL ALIVE.

When he walked into the room, slim, tall, blonde hair cropped short with piercing blue eyes - my heart contracted, as if it were a clenched fist finally peeling itself open to receive something. Receive love. I didn't mean to hold my breath, but I wanted nothing to come between us, not even my own exhalation. A loose thread that had been severed and dangling aimlessly inside me since the accident felt like it had finally found its other half and tied itself in a knot, without the need to utter a single word. Reunited.

So much importance is put on the spoken word; "Say what you mean" "Speak up for yourself" "Talk the talk" - all sayings I had overheard in the busyness of the hospital the last few days - but there is so much more to be said for the things that we *feel*. The things that don't need to be said. The things that *go without saying*. The things we just *know*. And I knew from one look that I love this man. I would say love at first sight, but I know I have seen this man before. Many times. Even if I can't quite remember when. Or where. But the electric charge hung between us in the air, almost suffocatingly strong. I could hear nothing but our hearts beating in the silence, in perfect unison, filling my eardrums.

He hugged me and I could not stop the tears from falling - an emotional waterfall, spilling out of me and onto him, saturating us both with feeling. It felt like coming home. Honestly, 10 minutes in his embrace made up for the previous days of loneliness, yesterday's emptiness easily whirrs in the background with only one thing in my mind. Him him him.

Its 5pm here currently and I really think I may go to bed for the evening NOW, to give my brain the decency of allowing its full power to focus on him and him alone, without energy being wasted on anything else (talking, walking, eating, peeing!) Oh Brain Power, please give 100% of your efficiency to him and him only. Forget my limbs. Forget my hunger. Even forget my healing. Focus fully on a daydream of him and him alone. And if I see him in my dreams while I fall asleep, (for the full 3D experience, of which only half of daydreaming can reach) then do so. I demand it. I will do nothing else to allow you to do that fully. I wont even move.

There is nothing in this world that I wouldn't give right now for him to be back. Not even myself.

Before he left, he promised me he would be here every day to see me. He didn't mention my disfigurement. He didn't mention our life - but that can wait. We have all the time in the world. And I will see him tomorrow.

"He is all that matters" my brain whispered to me in my own head.

"Now it will be ok".

filled with tears, mirroring my own. It was a blur, but a happy blur. An all consuming mindblowing blur. I really can't believe it. I wish he was still here.

When the time came for him to leave, I felt broken and have been in a fog ever since. I feel like a black cloud has been left behind, hovering right on top of me, suffocatingly pushing itself into every tiny crack of my brain and limbs, making it difficult to breathe, to think, to live. The nurse has been into the room asking me more insultingly boring questions but she felt so distant to me when she was talking, she may as well have been on the other side of the world. There was definitely a time delay between the words leaving her mouth and hitting my brain; all I could (can?!) think about is him him him. Im going through all of the necessary (boring) living and breathing motions of life on complete autopilot (talking, walking, eating, peeing!) while my brain incessantly eclipsed by his presence. Nothing else matters to me now, only him. Only this.

I suppose looking back he was rather quiet but I don't mind. We didn't really need to talk as looking at him told me everything I needed to know. It was bigger than words. I can see that our history is written on every inch of his face; the soft wrinkles by his telling blue eyes of years gone by, the laughter line markings of good times shared, a hand that fits perfectly into my own like ying and yang, as if made from the same mould. I know I share my life with him. I know I love him deeply and he loves me. I still have no idea who he is, or who I am but the comfort of it all was like looking in a mirror and seeing everything I needed reflected back at me. I know he is the other half of me, of my soul. I am certain.

He did tell me I'm beautiful (which is a surprise considering my face is horribly damaged right now but I will take the compliment all the same!) and he stroked my hair, his eyes

Chapter Fifteen

Him

The thing with me and Cecelia is that we are undeniably deeply bound together. Over the years whenever we have been apart it hasn't lasted long with both of us feeling the invisible magnetic pull back to each other and understanding over time that somehow without each other we are only worth half of what we were meant to be whole.

She spent 18 days at a silent retreat once wanting to fully "find herself" in the silence. It was part of a new age hippy movement she was heavily involved with at the time that I always thought promoted outlandish behaviour as "enlightenment" with spending more than two weeks in silence being just one of their schemes, but Cecelia was always much more spiritual than I was. She always had some 'other-wordly' reason as to why things were happening in every day life. "Its fate", "It's just meant to be" and "what's meant for me will never pass me by" became inarguable slogans she adopted when things around her fell apart -which they often did. Chaos attracts chaos and I always felt that her reaching out to " the universe" for answers was always just another way for her to abscond responsibility for many situations she caused - but it was always easier to let her carry on. Arguing with Cecelia never ended well for me. It was always easier to look the other way.

I always had a much more practical view of the world. Things were black and white. Simple. I just couldn't survive for long without her and that was the fact. I never really knew why but I was never much of a man, in my own mind at least, and without her I felt half less. She was dynamic enough to make up for it. Sometimes too much.

The first few days that she left for the retreat were absolute bliss for me. I revelled in the peace that being alone gave me and I found it amusing that *her* leaving to seek silence had actually given me the only quiet time I had experienced in months (she loved to talk).

But as the end of the first week beckoned, that slow lingering need for her to fill the gaping hole within me started to return and I began to count the days until she was back home with desperation, eagerly yearning for her fast talking and high volume voice to ricochet off the walls and engulf me once more.

By the end of the second week, all other time around the date of her return seemed to only exist as a prelude to that anticipated main event and every heartbeat became just one thud closer to seeing her again. I tried to fill the days with as much activity as I could to avoid even thinking of her but every quiet moment that arose, my brain would desperately flail around looking for a subject to clasp on to and would always land on thoughts of her in an attempt to fill the monstrous void of her actual presence. I was always unable to shake her out of my brain for long, even if I wanted to - we were intertwined and always would be. I always preferred to be unhappy with her close than happy with her away.

Seeing her at the hospital for the first time after the accident was emotional but also drastically uncomfortable for me. I could see the gleeful expectation in her eyes as soon as her gaze locked onto me and I could feel the disappointment ooze from her that I hadn't been there sooner. I was so massively aware of the magnitude of my visit and the surmounting pressure of my presence that washed over me so aggressively it nearly drowned me. She was always the one in charge. She was always supposed to be. It felt alien and suffocating to be the one on whose hopes were now pinned.

The dynamic was a shift I wasn't used to, and not one I would have openly chosen.

To describe her that day, she looked a lot cleaner than when I saw her straight after the accident but physically she was barely recognisable. Under the hideous facial disfigurement she looked pale, washed out, and the only colours on her stark white body were the deep black and purple bruises pressed into her skin as a reminder of their dominance, unwavering and unashamedly making their presence (and what had happened) well known to anyone who looked. Her usual wavy blond hair had been partly shaved and scraped back off her face, heartlessly displaying the severity of her new facial disfigurement with unwarranted pride but her wounds were much neater compared to the sickly gore I had encountered a few days before. She had always been beautiful with people always telling me that "she was the looker" of us both, then hesitating and stopping before saying that I was the brains (as the saying goes) as she was *very clearly* the brains too. But with the kind of brain she had always came the kind of disaster that always attached itself to intelligence. Her mind was always open, thirsty for knowledge and hungry for purpose. She was always reading and researching or spouting off some crazed new theory she had found online. Nothing was ever enough. Her eyes would flash with excitement and her words would take on an incredible pace, desperate to flow out of her and make their presence known in the world as unabashedly as she did. But her mind was almost *too* open, inside of her head holding *too* much space that left *too* much room for thinking, producing thought after thought after thought in an attempt to fill that open mind, like a production machine spiralling out of control. But seeing her there, on that hospital bed, her piercing blue eyes dimmed to blankness and her usual red smiley lips that had spoken a thousand insights now looking bloody and cracked, as if a single word would make them crumble, was the worst part of all. It was me that was forced into overthinking now. She looked so weak. It made me nauseous to see her like that. I told her she looked beautiful all the same. That's what cowards do.

Thankfully, that day Cecelia didn't ask me any questions and she seemed happy to receive my silence in exchange for my sheer presence. She spent a lot of the visit in tears, desperately grabbing my hand with a clasp so strong it served to remind me that her unwavering strength was still there, under the temporary weakness and hurt. I swear I could still feel her icy cold grip hours after I left that day and even after the physical sensation wore off, I could still feel her eyes boring into my soul with the look she gave me when I arrived. She spent the whole visit looking at me so intently I felt disgustingly exposed - like every hair on my body was being counted.

As was typical for Cecelia, any of the sparse conversation we had that day was directed completely toward her - how *she* felt, how *she* couldn't cope, how horrible the nurses were to her, how disgusting the food was. I was able to hide myself in plain sight behind her self-absorption, with her never ending mooning eclipsing my sunshine completely, allowing me the sanctity of darkness. But that part felt safe. Being the center of attention is one thing Cecelia was always good at - beaming the spotlight on herself - especially if she was the one in charge of the lights. I preferred to lurk in the shadows she cast.

That's why Amala and I clicked so much. It's impossible to compare both Cecelia and Amala. Not just physically, although the contrast is undeniably stark; Amala tall with her toned warm skin and long dark hair, perfectly sleek and put together - Cecelia blonde, bright, eccentric, beautifully unkempt. Amala was a lot like me in many ways; happy to be in the background and happy to watch the world go by but hers more from a quiet self assurance than mine which is birthed from my desperate desire to remain unseen. Amala gave me hope - that not everyone had to be loud, bright and brassy to hold a significant place in the world as Cecelia always made me feel that if you weren't constantly ablaze you were never going to set the world on fire. But Amala's elegantly simmering embers showed me another way. That there was beauty in the discreet. And once that fire started, I never wanted it to burn out. I never in my wildest dreams thought I would attract someone like Amala; someone who was happy for me to just be me and didn't constantly put me under the microscope under the guise of 'challenging me to grow". It was nice to feel important and Amala always did that. It's what drew me to her in the first place.

That and the variety. I had grown so tired of Cecelia. They do say variety is the spice of life.

Thankfully, on that first day at the hospital the hour of visiting time passed quicker than I had ominously inflated in my mind. It felt familiar - even though she looked like a stranger and our dynamic was outside of the norm she was very clearly still the same Cecelia underneath. She claimed to not remember anything at all, but the deepness of me was vast enough to hold all of our memories. And I would never forget.

But It's what would come next that scared me. When she would finally remember.

Chapter Sixteen

Her Diary - Entry 7

So I haven't been able to pick up this diary for a few days as I have been so FRUSTRATED I can't even put it into words. Even now I just want to stab the pen into the page and leave it stuck there, poking upright out of the paper like the invisible dagger than im currently feeling wedged into my heart. The days are dragging on longer and longer in this horrible room and the air conditioning constantly humming is starting to make me want to pick off both of my ears and throw them out of the window. But of course, the windows are bolted shut. I only realised that yesterday. Apparently I don't deserve "fresh air" in this place. Either that or they are fully aware of how GRIM this hell hole is and know that if the window isn't bolted shut that anyone subjected to this room for long enough (like me) will just launch themselves out of the window in an attempt to spice up the monotonous day. Honestly. If my bones weren't already broken I would definitely consider sacrificing both legs for an attempt at getting out of that 5th story window and onto the grass. But alas : the bolts.

Yesterday, I got the courage to write something in here but just ended up scribbling a hole in one of the pages, deeper and deeper. To be honest, I wanted to draw a hole big and deep enough to climb through like a tunnel to escape this nuisance place which is frankly starting to play on my nerves. That fat nosey nurse didn't look happy when she flicked through today and saw I had damaged half of the notebook and smudged biro all over the sheets in the process. Fuck her.

The main point of my frustration is the fucking BOREDOM here. Yes He has visited *every day* for the last few days, but visiting hours are ONE hour only which is miniscule in comparison to the vast NOTHINGNESS that surrounds it. And just as I get comfortable with him being around, tick tock the clock strikes and it's time for him to leave. Today I begged the nurse to let him stay, just one more hour, minute second - but no. The clock has all the power. It tick tocks constantly, taunting me, reminding me it cant be stopped. It goes on and on and on with all of the control and we are slaves to it. Nothing and nobody can stop it. I practically screamed for someone to listen to me when he left, but I bet nobody could hear me over the ticking. The time is deafening.

And now I'm alone again.

But HIM. My gosh. That is definitely something to write about and it's the only reason that I picked up this book today. I can't keep it to myself any longer. No matter how small the time is - being with him is absolutely amazing. For the past few days he's sat at the bottom of my bed tentatively clasping my hand, nodding interestedly, gazing lovingly with affection smeared all over his face. He always looks so INTERESTED in everything I have to say (as opposed to the nurses who can't seem to stand being around me for long - idiots. (IF YOUR READING THIS AGAIN YES YOU) BUT I am starting to get the feeling that he is holding back. He talks more now, but I always feel like he's treading water, working hard to keep the conversations surface level whereas I want to dive deep into every part of his mind. Its boring in the shallow. But thats all I have right now and I just can't bring myself to challenge and cajole answers. Especially when I only have him for one hour. I don't want to waste that time by bombarding him with questions or say something that will push him away. I'm trying to stay positive but the nagging reminder that he didn't visit for the first few days weighs heavy on my mind and I'm petrified that he will disappear. I can feel it. As if one wrong move from me will push him away and I can't stop thinking about that immense possibility. Its like quicksand; the more I try to struggle and try to get out of the thinking, the more it pulls me in, suffocating me with worry. So I will smile and stay quiet for now - just to keep him coming back.

The nurses have assured me that my memory will eventually start to repair if I take it easy enough. "Don't push yourself Cecelia" "Take it easy Cecelia" but all I seem to be doing is 'taking it easy' – even an arduous trip to the toilet is met with bated breath. I don't know why. Maybe they are afraid I will wander into another ward accidentally on my way for a pee and frighten *someone to death* with my disgustingly burnt face. If I did, Surely that would be a positive? At least it would bump up the death rate here a little and free up some beds for new patients. They always say they are overcrowded. I've heard them moaning constantly in the corridors.

But injury wise, apparently, im "healing well". Still not well enough to be of any value, but a "trot to the toilet and complete a word search in one of the free magazines" kind of well. But underneath it's my mind that's still all over the shop. I just have absolutely no clue what is going on.

But back to him: HE is a welcome distraction and the only positive in my life right now that is keeping me going. For the past few days, our conversations have evolved into him telling me little stories of our years gone by. Apparently, when we were in our late teens, I lost a job in a café because I failed to turn up for work when my alarm didn't go off one morning – because he had used the alarm batteries for his games console and stayed up all night playing - a games console I had bought for him with my earnings from the very same job. It was nice, hearing that story, even if we laughed for different reasons. Him laughing reflecting on the warmth of the memory and me, laughing at the strangers he spoke about and their misfortune. I found myself laughing just to laugh and see him laugh and even just knowing that I am involved in his happiness, even if its a past version of me who I don't recognise or know, feels like fireworks. To be honest, his stories are nothing more to me than fairy tales that could be about anyone. It could be about Mickey and Minnie Mouse (who they keep playing on the TV in our ward, I mean REALLY?!) for all the attachment I feel to the people in his stories. But I suppose I know Mickey and Minnie Mouse better than myself at the moment; I have spent more time with them than anyone else.

So I may be devoid of current memory, and totally lost as to what is happening but one thing I am CERTAIN of - I am completely consumed by this man. I definitely feel as if we are programmed the same; the laugh, the stories, each well timed joke; even our movements (the small ones I can make without being in pain) are in sync. He told me he loves me today. I told him back. Funny how I can both feel like I don't know him, and yet I know every inch of him, at the same time. Soulmates.

Thank god I have him. I am so lucky.

Now I must sleep.

Chapter Seventeen

Him

A week after the accident Cecelia had started to get anxious. She showed little to no signs of mental recovery with her memory still as dilapidated as her appearance, which, at the time, I saw as nothing but a positive. Without seeing her beautiful face, it was easier to keep her at arms length. It hurt my heart to see her in such confused pain, but for selfish reasons, I had to stay focused on what I knew was best for me – maintaining an emotional distance. I tried my best on those visits, nodding where I was supposed to nod, smiling when I was supposed to smile, letting her talk over and over about herself while throwing in a couple of stories of years gone by, but it was so difficult to match the person with whom I had shared so much with, to the mess I saw in front of me. She was so amiable now - all I had to do was smile and I could feel the happiness radiating from her. It was an uncomfortable feeling - she was never this easy to please. It felt so needy.

Each visit I spent tentatively perched on the edge of her bed, trying my best to look appropriately relaxed and comfortable, but ready to spring to my feet and bolt out of there at a moment's notice. She always just lay there, bandages twisted, her sheets crumpled, matching the look on her crumpled face, and it had scared me. It had scared me how much she had changed and how hard her life was going to be from here on in. And it would be even harder without me there beside her. But what was I supposed to do?

In all honesty, I had found the juggling of Cecelia and Amala a burden since the accident. In many ways, the practicalities were easier, with Cecelia being confined to the limited visiting hours of 2pm-3pm, allowing me to pigeon hole that relationship in my mind, and focus guilt free on Amala for the rest of the time. But despite the physical ease, the emotional burden had seemed to inflate to an imaginable size. I felt responsible, heartbroken and scared all in one. It was starting to become impossible that I could make everyone happy and that inner people pleaser, the one that was so used to kicking in to protect me, to give me that safe, easy life, was becoming harder to maintain - somebody was going to be disappointed soon, and how long I could put that off for was starting to become a task in itself. More importantly, how long would Amala let me get away with the juggling before she wanted more? Before she wanted me to leave Cecelia forever? I always battled internally between the manly egotistical pride of having two wonderful women in my life, and the burden and hate for the limitations it brought. I always wished I only had one. But choosing was nearly impossible.

Amala would never put pressure on me to leave Cecelia. She was too cool for that. She was a goddess of a woman and I often felt unworthy of her. Unworthy of why she would want someone like me in the first place. It was so hard trying to keep Amala on side and to keep her believing in me, the GOOD me, that I always made sure I was when I was with Amala, which was an exhausting task in itself. I never wanted her to see the real me; the me that Cecelia knew. I always wanted her to see me as the best version of myself. A curated version I put a lot of effort into maintaining. I feared so deeply that if Amala saw all the bad of me, she would walk away. There was no greater feeling that seeing myself through Amala's eyes and seeing her adoration and love for me reflected in her face. The way she looked at me, the way she held me, the way she positively glowed when talking about me and us. That just wasn't something I ever wanted to give up. I wouldn't. It was too special.

But the pressure of the accident was making it all harder to maintain. Cracks were starting to show. I could feel that something was coming. And I couldn't help but feel like this accident was an opportunity for me to finally break free from the trappings of Cecelia and everything that came with her.

I was told very early on by the doctors that due to the complicated nature of Cecelia's medical history, that it was very important that Cecelia's recovery was handled slowly, carefully and under the supervision of medical professionals. By this I knew that they meant her mental health; her folder was as thick as two bibles and just as sacred and I was warned not to divulge too much information about our personal life on those visits and was encouraged to be only positive in her presence. I was explicitly told that any tumultuous revelations could have an adverse reaction in the recovery processes, particularly because of her history. Looking back now I wonder if they were a little scared of her, like I always was.

At first, being evasive and fulfilling their request was easy for me (I was used to pretending) but I slowly started to realise that Cecelia was the only person in my life who I DIDN'T hide from. She was my release. The only person I could actually lift the mask around and know she would always be there, whatever version of me I showed. And now that option wasn't there any more, as she now needed a curated version of me too, which meant the mask was never being lifted. I felt the weight of it bore into my face with immense pressure every single, suffocating me. There were days when I could literally feel the pressure behind my eyes, the difficulty in my breath, the force over my mouth making it a struggle to communicate normally, never feeling a release from the constant burden of *having to be someone to somebody.* Someone who wasn't my authentic self. And the pressure was killing me. I now had to censor myself in front of Cecelia just as much as I had to with everyone else and all of a sudden, she was of less use to me than she had ever been before. It made me unable to connect with her. It pushed me further away. She became useless to me.

The emotional dissociation was made easier still by Cecelia's diminishing appearance. It was no secret that she looked like a totally different person. Her once luxurious blonde locks shaved on one side of her head, around the wound, the bruising like punctuation marks on her porcelain skin, her blue eyes dulled of the shine. I kept my distance, not only emotionally, but physically – kept the hugs minimal, the hand holding became a tactile staple. I told her I loved her because I did. I do. It's hard not to love somebody you have spent all of your life with but she seemed so different. Like a stranger. I knew it even as I said " I love you" that it wasn't her that I loved any more. It was who she used to be.

And it was Amala I wanted.

Chapter Eighteen

Her Diary - Entry 8

I'm starting to feel worse, not better. The panic that started within me when I arrived as a tiny flickering ember, hopeful that something good would happen and douse it to smoke with a large splash of positivity, is now ablaze inside me engulfing and growing at an alarming speed every day. Even breathing is difficult. Surely I should remember something by now. Anything.

If I hear someone say they are trying to help me "jog my memory" one more time I am going to lose it. My memory needs to be running, sprinting, hurtling towards the finish line, breathless with all of its knowledge and history and fact. But its barely taken one step forward, let alone the esteemed "jog" they keep mentioning.

For the last two days the nurses and doctors have taken a much more 'proactive' approach in my 'recovery', subjecting me to no end of new exercises to try and kickstart the JOG. This morning, for example, they held up picture after picture of places and people, asking me if they "struck any chords". Chords?! What chord would you like it to strike nurse? C major? D Minor? How about I hum a verse of "I'm a little teapot" for you complete with actions and then you can scribble that on your little clipboard instead of hearing me say "no" over and over. I tried to turn it into a little game at first, seeing how many different ways I could say "NO I DON'T RECOGNISE IT" for each question but by the fifth card when I had already used no, nope and na (with nada seeming too frivolous even for me) my game felt as boring as the card exercise so I just violently shook my head over and over and over until they took the hint and put the cards away.

And time STILL keeps ticking. And panic keeps rising. Nothing is getting solved. Nothing is getting better. Who am I? What happened? Why won't they just tell me? They could just TELL ME who I am and I'll learn. Everybody learns who they really are at some point in their life - I could learn NOW. I could study myself like a project. I could be a scholar in ME. I could learn to be me AGAIN. IF THEY WOULD JUST TELL ME. Why do I need to unlock it myself when they are holding the key? Im desperately trying to crack the code to the padlock thats locked around my brain while they sit there smugly knowing the combination. Why don't they just share it??

He visited again yesterday, but this time, instead of the usual calm, collected hand holding and story telling he looked impatient and brisk as if our 1 hour meeting was an hourglass and he was waiting for the sand to drip down and fill rock bottom so he could leave. It broke my heart to feel that energy shift from him: these visiting hours are what I live for currently and I've been so careful not to press him so he doesn't get frustrated with me. He didn't SAY that's how he felt, obviously, but I have become so hyperfocused on every inch of him that I can just feel it. I can feel even a slight change in mood, or facial expression, or breathing. I just know something is wrong. The energy is off.

I couldn't really stop myself when I asked what was wrong three times but each time the "nothing" got more and more abrupt. I'm sure I saw him visibly wince when I stroked my fingers along his wedding ring while holding hands - He hadn't worn the ring before and when I asked, he said he had finally found it after misplacing it at home. Myself, however, am still jewelryless. They tell me all of my jewellery was cut off and disposed of during the accident recovery but I can still see the faded skin on my hands and wrists where any light had failed to touch the skin where my jewelry would have sat every day. It's the only evidence of my life before the accident and the only evidence that I had a personality. I had THINGS. Things that meant so much to me that I refused to remove them in the sunlight, allowing them to cast a pale shadow that lingers over my fingers and arms in sacrifice for their importance.

But something strange is happening. When he hugged me goodbye today I tilted my chin as if to kiss him on the lips but he regaled so quickly and the horror in his eyes was so evident that it cut through me like a blade. It was hard to miss the look of pure disgust that snapped into place on his usual placid face. I just don't understand it. It MUST be my damaged face, repulsing him. I can see the tip of the wound on my collarbone constantly in my peripheral view and if I trace my finger over my cheeks it sends shivers to the tips of my toes. The nurses removed the mirror from my room after catching me using it to stare at my wound for hours. They said it was to stop me "dwelling on the negative" but I think it was to avoid my gentle unstable self headbutting the mirror to bits and giving everyone 7 years bad luck. Although I'm not sure how much worse my luck can get right now.

But I feel so angry. How dare he recoil? I can't help how I look. I can't change it. Surely he loves me and every inch of me like I do him? And I have been so GOOD too. On my best behaviour allowing him to witter on and on about his stupid stories, laughing at his unfunny jokes, keeping the questions to myself, letting him flit in and out on this room an hour a day while I'm here for every single second. I'm so embarrassed! Iv been putting so much importance on his visits I've allowed it to consume me! To stop me from seeing clearly! IM STUCK IN HERE and he gets to gallivant around, and he can't so much as KISS his wife!

When he visits tomorrow I shall ask him what is going on. Tomorrow I want to know who I am.

Tomorrow I want answers.

Chapter Nineteen

Him

It reached the point where I desperately needed a break. I was off work already so that problem was solved with a one month sick note from the doctors for "family stress" saving me from the humiliation of facing everyone and having to combat their unnecessary nosyness masquerading as concern. Amala needed a break too and was very much ready to get away for a few days, just the two of us, without the distractions that were eating into my day. "Quality time" she wanted, just us, a nice hotel, some wine, some fresh air. "Nowhere far" she had said. "Just far enough" and I knew exactly what she meant. Away from Her.

Telling Cecelia I wouldn't be able to visit for three days became a mammoth task in my mind and fabricating a complete lie so as not to alert suspicion about my trip with Amala took on a life of its own. I had planned the conversation over and over, written notes, ran through every scenario possible, speaking the words both silently and choked out at volume, bumping over the lump in my throat. I knew exactly what I wanted to say but actually saying it was another beast altogether and before long I had inflated the situation to such a size it was too big for me to hold.

When the time finally came to tell her, I froze. Knowing how she would feel, being left all alone, grappling with the same feeling I felt every time she was gone for too long where it would overwhelm me to the point of silence. I knew telling her I was going away for a few days was the right thing to do and that I could even package the whole thing nicely in a lie, wrapped up with the neat little guise of a "work trip" and deliver it to her in way that she would gladly receive, but I just couldn't do it. I just couldn't bare to witness the disappointment in her eyes that were already devoid of so much feeling. I couldn't bare for her to think badly of me. I couldn't bare to let her down. I even considered cancelling the trip but when I saw Amala packing her overnight bag with excitement flurrying through her like confetti and slowing down just enough to make sure I saw her packing some lacy, barely there underwear under a bottle of prosecco, I couldn't bare to let Amala down either.

When we were 17, in the times where I had passed my driving test and Cecelia had no inclination to learn (in part due to me always being available to transport her around at her beck and call) it became the norm that I always drove her to and from work. At the time she was working at a petrol station just outside town, way off the bus route, often until late into the evening - which worked well around our school commitments but not so well in terms of my social life as I had to be on hand four nights out of seven to make sure she got there and back. I didn't really mind. Only when Cecelia would frequently be late to collect often leaving me parked against the petrol pumps well after midnight following an 11pm shift finish, while she waved through the window having an after work chat with the petrol station "gang", or she would decide to pop for a drink with them into the pub next door after work. She never told me this in advance of course, it just became part of the expectation. I collected her at the end of her shift time and I waited until she was ready. That was the deal.

But there was one time when I was due to collect her from outside the pumps at 11pm and on the way I accidentally had a flat tyre (an inevitable byproduct of humping a 1974 cavalier over a mountain road every single day). I called the petrol station, telling them to let Cecelia know I would be an hour late and after 30 minutes of figuring out (for the first time) how to change the tyre for the spare tyre in the back, I raced to collect her, filled with nothing but pride at mastering something I had never done before and excited to share my achievement with her. I was 30 minutes later than her shift ended but still way before the time she usually left when "time ran away with her".

It was the first, and only time, I was late.

Most people would have waited.

Most people would have stayed put or decided to partake in that after work chat that always happened every other pick up, making her later and later every time.

Not Cecelia. When she knew I wasn't going to be there on the expected time Cecelia walked. 8 miles in the pitch black darkness. No coat. No phone. I found her long after midnight ambling down the dirt track with a tear stained face, hyperventilating and shivering, nearly a mile in the wrong direction.

She refused to go back to work after that. She told me that her confidence had been shattered - 'how could she possibly feel safe there now, knowing that it may happen again?' That she 'would be abandoned?' I had tried to explain that it was beyond my control, that these things happen, it was only an hour and it couldn't be helped and had she just WAITED things would have been fine, but she quit nonetheless. She cancelled an upcoming music concert with all of her friends, citing "lack of money" as she no longer had a job and from then on anytime one of those songs came on the radio, she would exhale loudly and tell whoever was in earshot about the time I stopped her going to experience them live.

If I didn't call and tell her I would be late, she would never have known and skipped out after midnight like usual, unaware I hadn't been parked counting the minutes like I normally did. But when she knew, I paid the price for that lateness for a very long time.

So in the end I didn't say anything about my trip with Amala.

It was easier when she didn't know things.

I just left.

Chapter Twenty

Her Diary - Entry 9

I knew it. I waited and waited for 3 days. Nothing.

He hasn't been. He hasn't visited.

I knew my horrific face would put him off. I had repulsed him.

I pushed too hard. I had tried so hard not to.

I'm just too ugly to be loved.

Chapter Twenty One

Him

The downside of burying your head in the sand is that at some point, you have to come up for air or you will suffocate. Those 3 days away were absolute bliss. Myself and Amala drank wine, we talked, we visited the art galleries that I loved that I now visited less and less with Cecelia as her ever growing list of hobbies had spiralled on and on, taking over, while mine always stuck the same and got left behind. It was so nice to feel seen and loved and relax into the fact that I was finally able to make someone happy again. The smile on Amala's face all weekend was palpable. It spurred me on. It was the boost I needed.

Art has always been a passion of mine - it's what Amala and I bonded over - and art galleries are one of the only places in this world where I actually feel comfortable and safe enough to be myself. I seem to gravitate towards art like a beacon of peace and I'm always in awe of people who have the absolute confidence to display their innermost feelings permanently, on canvas or sculpture, for the world to dissect and pull apart. I always wished I had that confidence in my own emotions. I always feel hopeful that there are people that are.

Cecelia liked to come with me to galleries but she never interpreted art in the same way that I did and always chose to find some other-worldly spiritual element inside it whereas my interpretations were always much more basely emotional. I would find the pain and joy in the reality and she would always find the unpredictable in the intangible. I *know* that is what art is designed to do - to be divisive and emotive - but Cecelia's opinions were so large they left little room for anything else. I always loved art and how it would allow me to get lost within it - to lose myself for long enough to forget the pain that came with being me. Whenever she came with me I always resented her for taking that space away from me with her judgement.

But as much as I loved art, I never had the talent to actually create it. And that's where Amala came in. The first time we met she was splattered with paint, long dark hair tied gracefully from her face, a grin plastered from ear to ear and a well used paint roller in hand. She was working on a local youth project that was leading a group of teenagers into painting murals on the walls of a local housing estate that had just had a renovation, turning the boring buildings pink and neon and injecting into them a much needed lease of life. It had even made the news and had been publicised all over the country for its unique take on community living, which had impressed me even more. It was unlike me, but I struck up a conversation with her as soon as I saw her, lost blindly in the overwhelming interest I felt for her and her passion. It turns out that she actually lived in the housing estate they were painting, adding another layer of awe and artistic involvement that I admired as she literally got to live and breathe her art. We spoke easily for hours with Amala finding my perspectives on the abstract paintings just as fascinating as I found her. It was always so easy with Amala and when she invited me inside to see more of her creations, I couldn't say no. And that's where it began.

It was only on the drive home from our weekend away that the sinking reality of my life with Cecelia had kicked back in once again.

Amala could absolutely sense the difference in my mood between the trip and the return home and there's one thing Amala would never stand for and that was to feel the burden of Cecelia on her time. "You're obsessed with her" she had spat at me in the car, her words hanging in her air, the weight of them wrapped around us for way longer than they took to speak. She wasn't wrong and we both knew it. No matter what happened between myself and Amala, no matter how good and easy it was, I would never shake Cecelia. The history was too deep.

Building up to the accident, Amala had started seeing more and more the impact of Cecelia's ties on me and had experienced the sheer weight of her dependency. I had hidden a lot of it by pushing the stresses deep down into the bottomless pit of my gut but Amala knew by now that for me, being quiet spoke just as loudly to convey my discomfort as any words ever could. If I ever succumbed to the inner retreat inside my own head it meant my overthinking was so loud there was barely any space left for actual conversation. It took everything I had to hold myself together, to function as a "normal" human being. To not let the mask slip.

But Amala had seen the 20 missed calls from Cecelia when I was 5 minutes late to pick her up from work. She had seen me forced to bike across town when Cecelia had hidden my car keys for weeks as punishment for using too much petrol and "damaging the environment". And Amala had been there, lying next to me, when the phone call from Cecelia's therapist came in to inform me of the severity of Cecelia's mental state and that she was recommending her further help. I didn't have to open up for Amala to know what I was dealing with.

At the start, Amala had dutifully played the role as a distraction and as the comforting light in the darkness of my life but lately, the way she always held her breath, rolled her eyes and tensed her muscles at the mere mention of Cecelia was now just enough to let me know not to darken her door with many of those troubles. Cecelia was my problem to deal with and mine alone.

Until now, Amala, who was always full of her own interests and passions was always happy to run through my life on an adjacent road to Cecelias, allowing me to flit between the two directions on whatever journey I was able to make. But lately she had moved closer towards the notion of the road becoming a single lane; "You need to cut her off so we can finally be together and be happy" She had said one Sunday morning. "She is getting in the way of your happiness." I had not replied, choosing instead to let the words wash over me like a river, drowning me in guilt and saturating my capacity to talk, hoping the conversation wouldn't continue. Amala didn't dare press the conversation, knowing deeply that the discomfort of the topic would bring an inevitable shut down in me and the road that she so desperately now wanted to be ridden as hers alone, would end up leading to nowhere.

Chapter Twenty Two

Her Diary - Entry 10

I am completely and utterly baffled. How could we go from those amazing, intimate visits, to now - nothing? NOTHING. He still hasn't visited. The nurses have absolutely no clue as to why, which is even worse (although I wouldn't be surprised if they do know and just wont tell me, they keep everything else hidden from me). My mind keeps flitting from pure rage at being abandoned into anxiety and worry that something has happened to him. What if something HAS happened to him? What if he has been in an accident too? What if he is now waiting for me in a hospital room like I am waiting for him and neither of us can reach each other. We need to be together!

But what if he's not? What if he is completely fine and has just decided not to see me again. I wouldn't blame him - look at the mess I'm in. I'm hideous. And pushy. Asking him over and over what's wrong - I would run too. Or even worse, what if he has just forgotten about me? Like I'm nothing. A nothing that has just slipped his mind.

I asked the nurses if they could contact him to try to find out what was going on but I could see them exchanging judgemental glances. Poor Cecelia. On her own. No other visitors and the only one she had has run away. I honestly can not believe this is happening. I miss him so much.

I could tell on his visits he wasn't the overly emotive type but I thought what we had went deeper than that. There are some things - ENERGETIC THINGS - that you feel and need to feel instead of hearing. Just because he didn't utter many words of love, doesn't mean there wasn't a huge energetic charge between us, pulling us together. I could feel it. The bond there. How could he not feel it? Maybe he didn't feel it at all and I imagined the whole thing?

But surely not.

So how could he just sever this with his absence as well as silence? Why even visit in the first place to then disappear into nothing? Why give that hope to then pull it away? I didn't ever ASK for him to come - I would have been happier never seeing him and being completely unaware. That's the thing about this memory loss - I can't remember anything that happened *before I got here* to give this situation context (maybe this is normal behaviour for him?) but it does elevate and accelerate the few memories I do have since the accident and make them all that more bigger to deal with. Him and his visits are currently all I have to hold on to and are the only evidence of a semblance of my life, knocking around in the seemingly endless vacuity. I have played each visit with him over and over a hundred times to inflate them into enough substance to make up for the history of my life that my brain just can't seem to access anymore. The hours he has frequented my imagination far outweigh the hours I have spent in his physical presence and the reality of him is now a mere drop in the never ending vastness I have created of him in my mind.

It isn't normal.

I could relay to you here the full conversations we have shared on each visit and I have analysed them from every angle, desperately trying to find meaning in every facial expression and the intention behind every word. One of the doctors recently told me that with memories, every time you relive a memory *you are always just remembering the last time you remembered the memory* and not the actual memory as fact itself. So its now highly possible that due to sheer exhaustion I have warped each and every interaction with him into something barely recognisable from the reality. Like a convoluted chinese whisper of recollection. But that's all I have. It really is all I have.

It's starting to KILL me, being in this hospital. My treatment intensity has accelerated with workshops and exercises every single day but they are still treating me like a delicate little flower blowing in the wind whose stem could snap at any moment. I can literally feel myself wilting under the mundanity of it all.

However physically I feel stronger. I am happily able to walk around and find joy in doing so but there's nowhere really interesting (or accessible) to walk to. I have been allowed to walk to the hospital library (a depressing place in itself) and given the autonomy (wow how lucky am I) of selecting a few books to bring back to the ward to entertain me (and they have a lovely little spiritual section I keep getting drawn to) but when the days stretch before you with no end in sight, there's no amount of page turning that can get you there faster.

But they DO seem to be encouraging the walking (rather than holding their breath and ushering me back to bed which is where we were last week), which is refreshing. However, they keep trying to get me to go outside. "Fresh air is BRILLIANT for your mental health" they keep telling me, but let me tell you, there is nothing FRESH about me dragging my feet around the outer walls of this grubby little hospital. Half of it is coated in fumes from the panicked ambulances whipping into the bays and wheeling people out at a frantic pace and the other half is people haphazardly blowing cigarette smoke from the smoking area around the air like clouds of despair. Its not really my idea of FRESH. So no thank you. I would rather pace the halls and the wards but apparently I am "getting in the way" by doing that for six hours out of twenty four.

All physical improvements aside, my emotions are so dysregulated I hardly know myself (not that I know myself anyway. HAHA). None of my feelings hang around long enough for me to know if it is really ME. Am I angry? Am I upset? Am I ok? I flit between absolute empty helplessness and crying myself to sleep in a little ball, to absolute determination, wanting to jump up and run around the room to prove my healing, to the gut churning anger spitting out profanities to anyone who dares cross my path, to seemingly never ending sadness and loneliness and apologising for even existing. The mission here, apart from the obvious physical healing, is for me to remember who I am. But how can I focus on who I am if my temperament changes so rapidly, it's hard to know which one is the driving force. Which part of me is real and which one is the fleeting emotion? Which part of me is "out of character" when my character is so hard to hold on to? Am I an angry person, with moments of calm. Or a calm person with moments of breathtaking rage. It's so hard when you don't know who you are.

This week the big revelation for me has been guided meditation - something that has been introduced as part of my rehabilitation and the effects have been wonderful. YES it involves me lying down with my eyes closed after days of complaining that I want to stop being stuck in this bed sleeping BUT what I have found in my mind in those moments of meditation is worth the extra bed sores. Actual peace. Those moments of quiet, with the nurse playing a faint little zen audio on some ancient speaker that looks like it belongs in a museum amazingly actually silence my brain long enough for me to gain some hope within my situation. We started our venture into the meditation experiment last week with some nice basic audios to chill me out but since my quite obvious keenness for it, the nurses now allow me to choose my own audios for each session from a huge playlist of options. Some of them are nice and simple, with the sounds of rain or waterfalls but some of them are blowing my brain wide open! In yesterday's audio, some guy with the most calming voice I have ever experienced guided me so far into relaxation I felt like a white light was pulsing through the whole of my body and a happiness was present that I haven't felt in days. And in today's audio, for twenty whole minutes I was taken on a spiritual journey deep into my subconscious where I had the most wonderful conversation with a spirit goddess, who reassured me that everything would be ok.

These meditation moments have now become my new solace - the hopeful punctuation marks that break up the sentencing day, which used to be filled by his visits. Even if I have no visitors, and no hope, I now know I am divinely supported.

This folly into the spiritual has also helped me to start to understand all of the energetic feelings I KNOW are there between me and him. I read a fantastic book about Twin Flames from the library, and how it describes two souls that are believed to be halves of the same energy source, that have been been split into two bodies. A huge part of the twin flame concept is this period of separation they must go through and how they must be apart to come together stronger. Maybe this is what is happening here? Maybe this is why he has disappeared?

So I have to stay positive that he will return. Surely he will. The universe WILL align and bring us back together again, as I KNOW that we share the same universal path. We are bound together. One soul in two bodies. I just need to wait. Then it's my turn.

Chapter Twenty Three

Him

I suppose after the trip, it all started to get worse.

My bond with Amala had grown deeper and stronger since our mini break and we were better than ever, as long as we tiptoed around the Cecelia problem which was now the constant elephant in the room. There were times when I would immerse myself completely in the present moment with Amala and accidentally forget about Cecelia, before the crushing guilt and fear would hit me so hard out of nowhere it felt like all gravity had been removed from under my feet. All I could do to keep going was to ignore it. I know people say 'ignorance is bliss' but what they don't say is that bliss also comes with sacrifice. After a while, the ignorance itself almost took on a life of its own, growing bigger and more impossible to solve with every passing day and as time ticked on by, it was almost too far gone to put right. The elephant in the room had turned into a herd and they were ready to trample on me at any moment. I felt like I was underwater every single day.

Although I *knew* I should go and see her and comfort the closest woman possible in my life, it felt so much safer and easier to hide. It was too much fun to play pretend for a while and star in the role of the unburdened, happy, appreciated, in-love man with Amala. But I always knew deep down that it was temporary and Cecelia hadn't actually gone away. That she would always have to come back. She always did.

She couldn't stay in that hospital forever. She would eventually heal, on a physical level at least and I knew if I didn't go in and face the situation, she would find me and make me face it anyway. And that was the most terrifying thought of all.

Chapter Twenty Four

Her Diary - Entry 11

So there's talk of me being allowed out on a day trip. A DAY TRIP! OUTSIDE OF THE HOSPITAL! I am so excited I am a little scared to actually believe it is true so until I sign the forms and it is official, I am waiting with bated breath and am on my best behaviour until it does. Apparently they have taken on board my feedback that the hospital grounds are less than appealing for my much needed mental health walks and it seems that a nice long stroll around the local lake would do wonders for me all around. I would be chaperoned of course. I heard the nurses muttering in the corridor over "who has drawn the short straw" but I could be accompanied by a donkey for all I care, as long as I get a change of scenery. I couldn't care about the short straw, as long as I'm given one to drink in all of the excitement.

Still no visits.

But I will be out soon.

Chapter Twenty Five

Him

When my time off work turned into months rather than weeks, I found myself not only isolating from Cecelia and the hospital, but from human interaction in general. Without my daily routine forcing me to stick on that smile and exchange fake pleasantries with the office staff, I found that those pleasantries never came and the smile stayed permanently unstuck.

I had lost count of the amount of times I had picked up my phone to return the hospital's many missed calls, or slipped on my coat and loafers ready to make the journey to visit whenever a temporary bout of courage pushed me into action but it wasn't long before the fear kicked in and it seemed so much easier to just turn around, switch off the phone and use the coat and shoes to drag myself on a lethargic walk around the lake that surrounded my house instead, watching carefree dog walkers and teenage ball kickers with envy at their energy. Without Cecelia I felt stuck in no man's land. A limbo between relief and panic, my nervous system feeling so dysregulated at the lack of constant control and pressure that came from her presence that it had inevitably shut me down, turning me into a husk. I had no purpose, even if my previous purpose was less than happy, at least I felt I had one.

Still. I stayed away.

Amala was less than pleased at my new found demeanour, urging me to "get out" and "do something" or at least put things right with Cecelia if it was going to have this negative effect on my whole life - but I still couldn't face it. I wasn't used to being the one in control and without Cecelia's driving force behind me, I just couldn't make the journey forward. I couldn't go the distance.

At that point, I had far departed from the demanding juggle of keeping two women in my life happy to now easily pleasing neither. Amala had grown exasperated, treating my constant presence like a burden on her usual self sufficient schedule and my head was warped, with the last image of Cecelia burned underneath my eyelids staring back at me every time I dared to close my eyes, looking weak and frail and helpless and disappointed.

Cecelia and I had always been able to strangely tune into each other, even in times of absence and there were many times where she would be out with her friends, or away on a trip and I just *knew* that something was wrong, or that something bad was going to happen. More often than not I was right but I suppose that becomes par for the course the more frequently it happens - chaos almost becomes expected when it starts to become the norm and maybe it wasn't a mystical hunch at all. It was inevitably Cecelia being Cecelia everytime

But I couldn't help listening to this deep nagging feeling inside me that she was out there, getting stronger every day and when I would see her next she would be a far cry from the frail, harmless and helpless person I saw on my last visit. She wasn't that person and I needed to remember that and not get sucked in. I needed to stay strong.

I needed to stay away.

Chapter Twenty Six

Her Diary - Entry 12

THE DAY IS HERE! TODAY I FINALLY GET TO GO OUTSIDE!

At 11am today, the nurse with the brown hair and the dodgy highlights is taking me to Lake Elid for a 45 minute outing consisting of a coffee, some well needed fresh air and some adult conversation. Im unsure why a lake has been the destination of choice but I heard the nurses say something about the lake being close enough so that they didn't have to "drag this out for longer than necessary" but when I asked them outright, they said it was chosen for its 'scenic views and stimulating sensory areas that would be fantastic for my mental and physical wellbeing'. Liars.

But who cares? I AM GETTING OUT!

After a 30 minute safety briefing after breakfast I have been extensively pre warned that the lake is next to a housing estate which is known for its busyness and to take it at my own pace. Apparently it's a bit of a local tourist attraction known for its tall multicoloured buildings and coloured murals on the walls as part of a local youth project. I think they are afraid that my brain will combust after weeks of seeing the same five people and grey walls on loop but the thought of seeing OTHER PEOPLE and feeling some normalcy is setting me on fire! I have been told that if I feel overwhelmed, or the area feels too hectic I am to tell the nurse and her dodgy highlights that I want to go back to the hospital immediately (as if thats going to happen!). However, after noticing the ice cold death stare I gave them when they were sucking all of the fun out of this trip with their moaning, they also extensively reassured me that the buildings next to the lake have so much exciting art and painted murals on them, that I will find the visit really rewarding. "A sight for sore eyes" they had described it as, but it's not my eyes that are sore. It's my heart.

Clearly he still hasn't visited. And the pain is unbearable.

As exciting as this trip is, I can't quash the burning desire inside me for him to be on this day trip with me and to share this moment together. We could walk hand in hand, the breeze twisting around us while his arms twist around my waist, deftly guiding me around the lake, pointing at the murals, smiling and the ducks enjoying each others company.

Oh how I wish so much that he was here now. My heart aches for him.

But enough of that for now.

I'M GETTING OUT!

Chapter Twenty Seven

Him

At this point I am lost for words.

I really am.

I knew something terrible would happen.

I could feel it.

Chapter Twenty Eight

Her Diary - Entry 13

When the day finally arrived for me to go outside, I could hardly contain my excitement. After days and days of nothingness, the sheer promise of possibility was almost too big for me to comprehend. I was dressed and ready to go at 7am, even though we weren't leaving until 11am - I just could not wait. My impatience exacerbated further when the nurse who was "chaperoning" me was 8 minutes late to collect me (I counted) but nonetheless, my spirits were not dampened for long. Even during the 6 minute taxi ride where she made me sit in the back on my own while she chatted haphazardly to the taxi driver in front I only felt temporarily insulted before the excitement forced its way out as today's predominant emotion. I was so happy to look out of the window and drink in the sights and wiggle my bum cheeks into a different chair after weeks and weeks of being subjected to the rock hard foam of the hospital cushions. It was so refreshing to look at something other than the four white walls that had enveloped around me, keeping me trapped for the last few weeks.

It's surprising how the little things you take for granted in life become the very things you crave when they are taken away. A simple drive, a walk, some fresh air and I was content. I had probably walked this route a thousand times before, head down, engrossed in my daily activity, annoyed that the traffic was so bad and cursing the very road I was now filled with gratitude for. A change in perspective is a beautiful thing. I don't think I stopped smiling all morning.

And then it got even better. Not even being forced to walk laps around the lake arm in arm with the nurse like some sort of prisoner could deter me from the magic. It just felt wonderful to be outside. It's a funny little park really. All of the houses are painted a different colour and the grounds around the lake are filled with art projects, like one in particular that caught my eye; a giant paper mache pink elephant covered in handprints from the local primary school. I never thought I would be the kind of person to weep over something so twee (lets be honest - all art made by a child is shit unless its from your own spawn, where I imagine your love for them is so gigantic it eclipses the rubbish they proudly create and inflates your pride in return) but im not ashamed to say it brought tears to my eyes.

But then it all got a bit weird. The park was quiet, as expected mid morning on a weekday, apart from a few geriatric dog walkers and a handful of panting joggers in their sweatpants, incessantly checking their fitness watches. At first I was completely consumed by all of the things to see around me but all of a sudden, it was as if I felt the wind change. Suddenly, the cooling breeze which I had refreshingly welcomed through my hair and cheeks mere moments before now felt sharp and biting, as if it had slapped me across the face.

Turning to see a bicycle zoom through the grounds at a rapid rate really was something to catch your eye. Even more so when it was ridden by a 6ft blonde man, his hair cropped short, his eyes sparkling in the wind.

At first I thought there was some sort of mistake. It couldn't be him. Surely not this close to the hospital, a mere few miles down the road. Surely he would have visited me more if he was hung around this close. It just didn't make sense. What was going on? My heartbeat was so loud I was POSITIVE he would hear it hammering from across the lake and turn towards the noise, just to see me there and run over and explain. There must be some sort of mix up. I just didn't understand.

But it WAS him. I could see him more plainly as he peddled up to one of the pink coloured houses and turned to mount his bicycle against the wall. Here he was! At last! My confusion became quickly eclipsed with absolute JOY as I realised my manifestation of being in the park together, of holding hands, of having coffee, was about to become true. I knew it! I knew I just had to be patient and believe it! Thank you Universe!

I thought for a second that maybe this was some sort of organised surprise just for me - that the nurses had arranged. How horrible could I be, being rude to them over and over and all along they were planning a surprise for me! I thought they must have finally got in touch with him, straightened out the mix up of his failed visits and arranged for him to meet me here. I thought it was all for me and it took everything in me to stop myself screaming - He is here! He is here! HERE I AM!

But before I was about to break into a run, ready to shorten the distance between us to nothing and to put an end to the surprise, I saw her.

I saw the same biting wind blow her dark hair away from her shoulders as she opened the door, revealing a sickeningly happy grin.

I saw him reach for her face, tucking the hair behind her ears and cupping her chin towards his.

I saw her tilt her head towards him, eyes closing with happiness.
And I saw him kiss her. Right there. On the doorstep.

And then I saw red.

Chapter Twenty Nine

Him

To know now, that her visit outside was willingly organised by the medical team, makes me lose complete faith and respect in the NHS. How was that allowed to happen? With her history of mental issues? She should have been kept inside, kept safe, kept AWAY, until everything had been done within their power, to ensure she was of sound mind. They tell me the whole visit and location was planned to slowly introduce her to familiar places. They KNEW I lived there. They KNEW I was staying away from her because I knew how volatile she could be. And instead they brought her to my door.

And now look what's happened : my lovely amazing beautiful wife is dead. She's dead.

I blame her. Of course I blame her. But I also blame them.

Chapter Thirty

Angus Day, the police officer on duty, shuffled his lengthy written notes and rubbed his temples; tired after 6 hours of interviewing Oliver Tamsin. He had definitely drawn the short straw today, he thought. He was supposed to be counting down the hours until his annual leave, which kicked off in approximately 3 hours, but then this case had been called in and, due to staff sickness, he had been drafted in to conduct the interview. He hated interviews. It was the most boring part of his job. Especially when it was with people like Oliver Tamsin, who had the personality of a flea. But a girl was dead and the interview needed to be conducted. It was the worst part of the job.

Angus leant back in his chair, wondering how he could discreetly check the time on his watch without making it obvious that he was counting down the seconds until his shift was over. His wife, Eleanor, was at home waiting for him, with their newborn baby, Lucas. He had promised her he would be home on time today, to take over from nearly three weeks of sleepless nights which were taking their toll on the both of them. Not even the three black coffees on this shift could switch off the tired vein that incessantly thrummed on his temple throughout the duration of the interview. To be honest, he hadn't really been concentrating for the last few hours, worrying about Lucas, and colic, and Eleanor and her tear stained face that gaped after him as he had left this morning. The last month had been tough to say the least. He was hoping the tape recorder that had been running throughout the interview would pick up the slack. Modern technology would capture the words, he was just there to facilitate it.

Angus took two loud slurps of coffee, one after the other, and prepared himself for the closing question, the one that was going to wrap this interview up, and allow him to get home. He couldn't even remember the names of the people in question, he had to keep checking his sheet in front of him, where the words swam around like flabby fish.

And then he asked it.

"So Oliver. What final words do you want to give about your wife and her mental state?"

The flicker of confusion in Oliver's eyes had thrown him. It was supposed to be a simple question, an attempt to summarise a long six hours. Angus flicked through his paperwork once more. Yes, Oliver was definitely married. His eyes flitted to his finger, relieved to see him displaying a wedding ring with pride.

"My wife's mental state, officer? Is that a sick joke?" Oliver's voice both hard and wavering at the same time.

Angus frowned, the words on the page becoming even more confusing, her heartbeat quickening, unsure if it was from the coffee or the sudden change of atmosphere in the room . He couldn't mess this up. Not now. He was so close to clocking out.

"Yes, your wife Mr Tamsin. She has an intense history of mental illness. Cecelia?"

Angus gulped. He was sure he had her name right. He had been listening to Oliver talk about her incessantly for the last 6 hours.

"Cecelia??" Oliver recoiled in horror.

"Cecelia is not my wife officer. She is my sister."

Chapter Thirty One

Her

He always thought he was better than me. Do you know how fucking annoying it is to be one half of a whole, your WHOLE life. You couldn't even have a womb on your own. You were brought into this world as a twosome and to be physically incapable of surviving without another human being is a god damn hindrance if I ever saw one. I never asked to be a twin. It was forced upon me.

We managed fine through school and our young adult years - we were a life line to each other I suppose. Many times I tried to break free from the suffocating noose that his existence constantly hung around my neck, but I always got drawn back in. You never know love and hate until you hate half of yourself.

Literally.

He was always a wet blanket. No ambition. It was disgusting. Always hanging around waiting to collect me from work at my beck and call, even if I made him wait over an hour in the hope that he would get the hint. I had to stop working in the end - I couldn't deal with him hanging around, insisting on collecting me. I would often give him the wrong times so he would finally understand he wasn't wanted but he would find me and take me home. There was no escape. No solace.

And then our parents died and the codependancy was elevated to another level. It was just us, alone and intertwisted.

I booked my travel tickets for an around the world adventure twice for him to realise I wanted to branch out on my own but it was never enough for him to take the fucking hint. The guilt held me back. I booked an 18 day silent retreat once just to have some god damn space after nearly 20 years of his incessant lingering, both around me and inside my head. It was like we shared a consciousness. But even the distance didn't stop him from being inside my head. That's the problem when you develop a brain at the same time, in the same place.

And then he met her. Amala. And he became insufferable.

Smiling and whistling around the place, it's like he had achieved a level of happiness neither of us had ever accessed before. And we were safe in our misery together. How dare he be the one to break that unspeakable pact. I tried to end things for myself many times, failing miserably and spending weeks on end in rehabilitation centers being pumped with various medications to combat my depleted mental state. But I knew that nothing would stop it. It was him. He was the problem. And even moving away wouldn't solve it - he was always the other half of me. I wanted to be whole.

It got to a point where I would despise seeing my own face in the mirror, as all I saw staring back at me was Him. We shared the same eyes, the same nose, the same face, the same slow lazy walk. But now, since he met her, his eyes twinkled, his face held a certain glow of hope and his lazy walk had an undeniable skip in its step. It was then I knew that the both of us couldn't survive. Couldn't thrive. It was him or me. No more half.

This time, I tried to end things for myself again first. Selfless as I am. That's why I threw the burning fat over my face from the steaming pot in the restaurant while I worked and threw myself backwards down the kitchen stairs. An "accident" they have called it continuously over these excruciating months in my "recovery". There was no accident at all. The only accident is that I didn't drown myself in it enough. It was impromptu really, even though the sentiment had been there for a while. I caught a glance of my face in the mirror and all I could see was Oliver's face looking back at me. And all of a sudden melting it off seemed a fantastic idea. Thats the fucking problem with being a twin. Nothing is your own. Not even your face.

But when my latest half assed suicide attempt failed and I was brought to the hospital, I knew then that this was my final opportunity to make something of the situation before I was detained once again in some psychiatric facility. Maybe I wasn't the one who needed to go after all, and it could be him instead. Maybe this was my chance. To get shot of him forever.

Using a failed memory seemed like the perfect alibi. The stupid nurse with the blonde highlights practically handed it to me on a plate when the first line she uttered to me was "You're going to be ok. Do you know where you are? Do you know your name?". It was the perfect fucking crime, delivered to me first class by the NHS. I definitely would be standing on my doorstep clapping for that.

And from there it all snowballed perfectly. Oliver, being his usual flakey, non committal self walked straight into the trap of bailing on me and evading the nurses, allowing me to fully play into the sad girl act. I knew he would. Oliver always hated hospitals after years of trying to rescue me every time I was brought in. I knew the effect they had on him and I knew deep down he was as desperate to get rid of me as I was of him.

So the sad girl act worked a charm. I was the sad girl who had nobody. The sad harmless girl that needed fresh air. The sad girl who always complained she had nowhere to walk or go. The sad girl who secretly knew that there were no other scenic places nearby except the local lake, directly opposite Oliver and Amala's house and with the current strain on the NHS staff, I was the sad girl who knew the quicker the day trip the better, making it the perfect location. They hadnt lived together in that house for long - it had always been hers but he had moved in a few weeks after their wedding. WHY he chose to do that always escaped me. Who would want to live in a house painted like a nauseating children's TV show. One of her "amazing projects" he kept saying. The house should be burned to the ground to save unsuspecting people like me from having to look at its hideous decor. Maybe that's what I should have done.

But this option just "arrived" on my doorstep, and who was I to turn it down? I took it as a nudge from the universe - the perfect alibi. Who would blame me for being confused? With my history of mental illness. We had the same surname, he wore a wedding ring, my disfigurement made the identical twins part non existent. If I played up my mental state big enough, I knew nobody would correct me and be afraid of triggering me even further. Poor sad disgruntled wife, stuck in hospital while she thought her "husband" was off having an affair. I could plead insanity. I could blame the trauma, the heartache, his absence and "infidelity" as my reasons. I could blame my confusion. I could blame misinterpretation of our bond. That I thought our bond was more twin flame than twin brother. We shared a surname after all. I wasn't that far of a reach. You could usually spot the identical features a mile off and put two and two together when you saw us in the same room but with my recent advancement on the disfigurement front, nobody would immediately know. And more importantly, I can play that I MYSELF DIDN'T KNOW. The newspapers would write about it "poor heartbroken wife suffers traumatic accident to find out her husband is having an affair". NOBODY would blame me. And I could get rid of him forever.

Well. That was the plan.

I didn't expect to kill Amala instead.

Chapter Thirty Two

Him

Cecelia always found being a twin difficult. We both did, especially because we looked so alike but were so opposite in every way. It's so difficult to describe what it feels like having a twin. The bond. The tie. You literally cannot live without that person, even if you don't want them in your life. Even If you hadn't shared a womb you wouldn't even entertain each other's company.

Cecelia always had a problem with Amala and Amala found it hard, being second best. Cecelia was the first woman in my life, the other half of me - they say blood is thicker than water but we did not only share blood. We shared a womb. It was hard. I tried to prioritise Amala, I tried to cut the ties. But I always felt lost without Cecelia close by. That's what happens when you are one side of a coin. No matter if it lands on heads or tails, the other side is still there waiting to be flipped.

Cecelia has always had issues. Always struggled mentally. We were so connected it troubled me at times to feel her pain. Hear her anguish. Live her troubles. I had tried to help her many times, but there was a broken part of Cecelia that just couldn't be fixed. Not even by me, who had all of the tools to complete her.

I think that's what Cecelia always struggled with. We shared the same blood pumping through our veins, a womb, dna. We shared the same eyes, the same nose, the same walk. I could feel and hear her thoughts, I could sense every fibre of her make-up without her speaking a word. And we had shared a life for the first 20 years, just us. But with Amala - she was my soulmate. Our bond, in many ways, was just as intense. With Amala I shared a soul, we shared hopes, we shared dreams. And Cecelia was unable to compete.

I never thought it would get this far. When I heard she had another accident, I thought it would be the same old story. A few weeks and she would recover, a few months she would be in high spirits, lapping up the aftermath of the attention, and then she would dip again. It was a pattern we had experienced many times before. Amala has already checked out from it. She had hit her "Caring" capacity years back. It's why I tried so hard this time to not let this accident consume me. Why I tried to stop the initial shock and despair from pulling me back into Cecelias trap. It's why I didn't visit. It's why I prioritised Amala. It's why I tried to distance myself from the never ending weight that Cecelia bares on me. It's why I tried to break free.

But she got her way in the end.

And here we are.

Chapter Thirty Three

Newspaper Article

"Disfigured young woman kills twin brothers wife in Elim Park; the land of the famous REBORN Youth Projects, which she helped to develop"

A young woman, with a history of severe mental illness, has been arrested today for the murder of her twin brothers wife, Amala Tamsin. Cecelia Tamsin, recently admitted to St Elim Hospital for severe injuries following an accident at work, was out for the day on respite, chaperoned by a nurse from the facility, when the murder occurred, where a large rock from the park grounds, was thrown directly as Amala Tamsin, who was stood on her doorstep with her newly married husband, and twin of the accused, Oliver Tamsin.

In a slight twist of fate, Amala Tamsin, famous locally for her charity and youth work in the Elim area, ran several youth projects over the last five years in the exact park that has now become her place of death and it it is speculated locally that the rock that was used as the murder weapon, was part of an art feature that Amala Tamsin had recently completed with the local teenagers of Elin Secondary School.

The local police are investigating and our thoughts are with the family at this heartbreaking time."

Chapter Thirty Four

Her

It was just too brilliant. The sheer incompetence of the nurse with me. The opportunity that arose.

They always say about twin telepathy, it was one of the most asked questions we always had when we were young. "Can you read each other's minds?". The answer was, of course, no, but there was something so much bigger than that. You could FEEL each other, sense each other, pick up on vibes that nobody else could. And most importantly, you could always tell when you were near each other.

I knew that day, as soon as I put a foot into that park, that Oliver was on his way to his house. I could sense it. And the nurse happily let me peruse the area, hoping that it would "help my memory" being close to home and mistaking my darting eyes that were looking for any sign of him, for the wonder of being out in the elements, finally, after weeks of being locked inside. That wasn't the case.

And when I saw him, metres away from me, kissing her on their doorstep, before she was about to mount her bicycle that was propped up outside their sickeningly painted house, It all hit me like a freight train I couldn't control. So I picked up the rock, and I threw it.

I never had a good aim.

THE END

Printed in Great Britain
by Amazon